BEARS
CAN'T PLAY SOCCER!

written by
Beth Thompson

illustrated by
Roksana Oslizlo

ISBN 978-1-9164680-4-7

First Edition

For Charlie Bear,
my soccer-crazy son.
-B.T.

It was cup final day for the junior soccer league.
The bottom of the league, the **Red Dragons**,
were playing the top of the league, the **Mighty Wasps**.

At half-time the Dragons were five-nil
down, with three injured players
and no more subs left to play.

As the whistle blew for the second half,
a dark shadow appeared over the pitch.

"IT'S A MONSTER!"
hollered a Dragon.

"NO, IT'S AN ALIEN!"
cried a Wasp.

"IT'S A B...B...B...BEAR!"

screamed the referee, and he dashed off
the pitch as fast as he could.

The bear stomped onto the pitch, **grunting** and **growling**.

He sniffed the ball and then flicked it up into the air, juggling it between his head and his snout, his knees and his paws.

Then the bear **kicked** the ball right over his head, over the halfway line and straight into the Wasps' net.

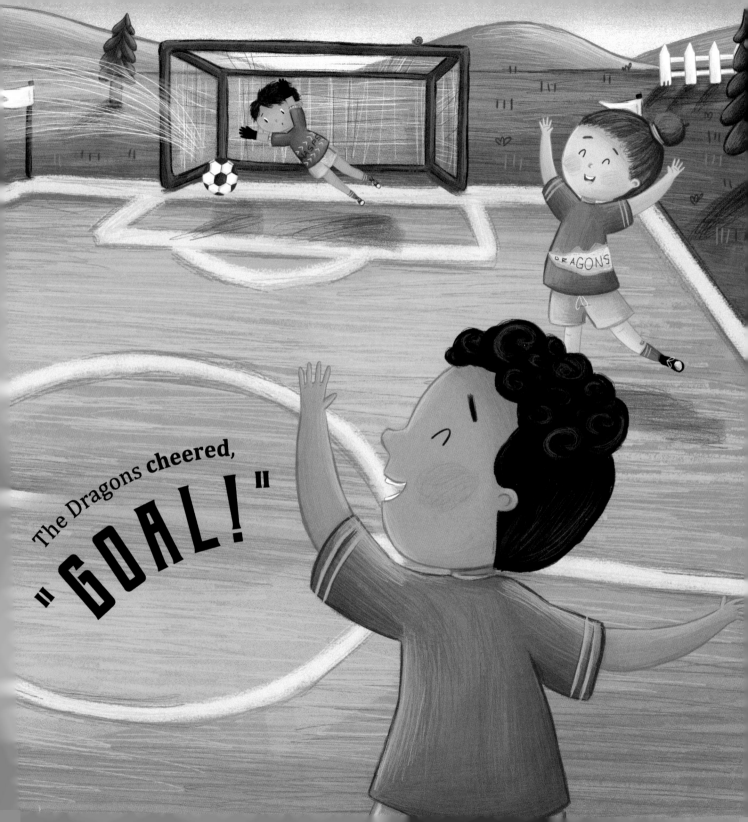

The Dragons cheered, "GOAL!"

The referee crept out from his hiding place and blew his whistle.

"Bears **can't** play soccer," he protested. "Goal disallowed!"

The Dragons' coach flicked through her rulebook but found no mention of bears anywhere at all.

"Goal allowed!" sobbed the referee.
The Dragons cheered.

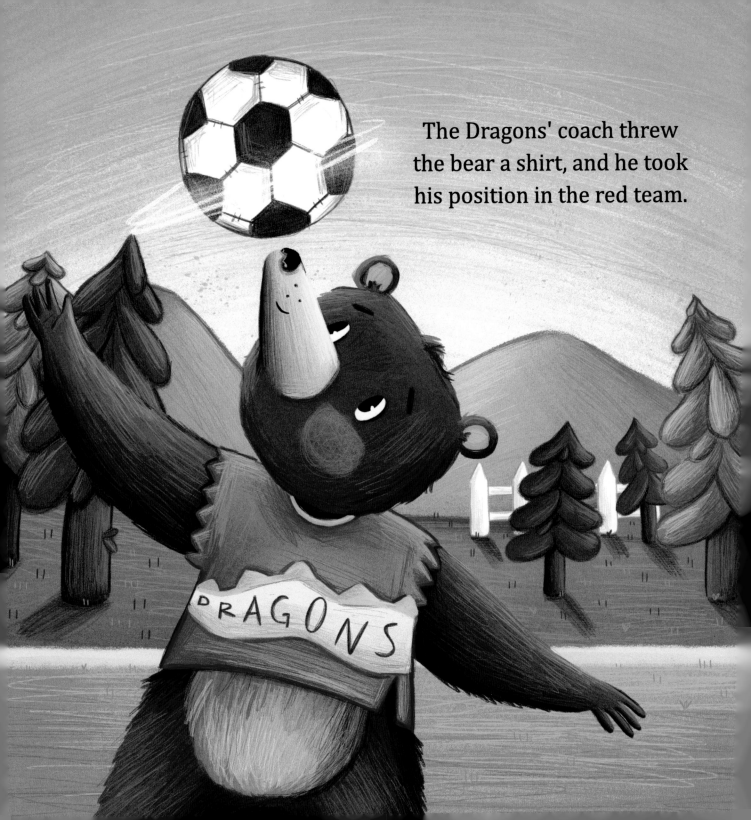

The Dragons' coach threw the bear a shirt, and he took his position in the red team.

The whistle blew. A Dragon passed the ball to the bear.

With some nifty footwork, he swept past *one, two, three* Wasps before lobbing it into the net.

"GOAL!"

5-2

The bear **leapt** and **bounced** across the pitch, passing and dribbling the ball past the Wasps, scoring again, *and again, and again.*

"GOAL!"   GOAL!"
"GOAL!"

The score was five-five with one minute left to play. The referee blew his whistle.

A brave Wasp **tackled** the bear, and
the bear tripped and fell to the ground.
"Penalty!" cried the referee, and he sent
the Wasp off with a red card.

The bear stood on the penalty spot.
He hesitated, and then walloped
the ball straight into the top corner.

The bear dived to the floor and slid
across the pitch as the whistle blew for full-time.

The Dragons won the cup final,
all thanks to the mystery bear.

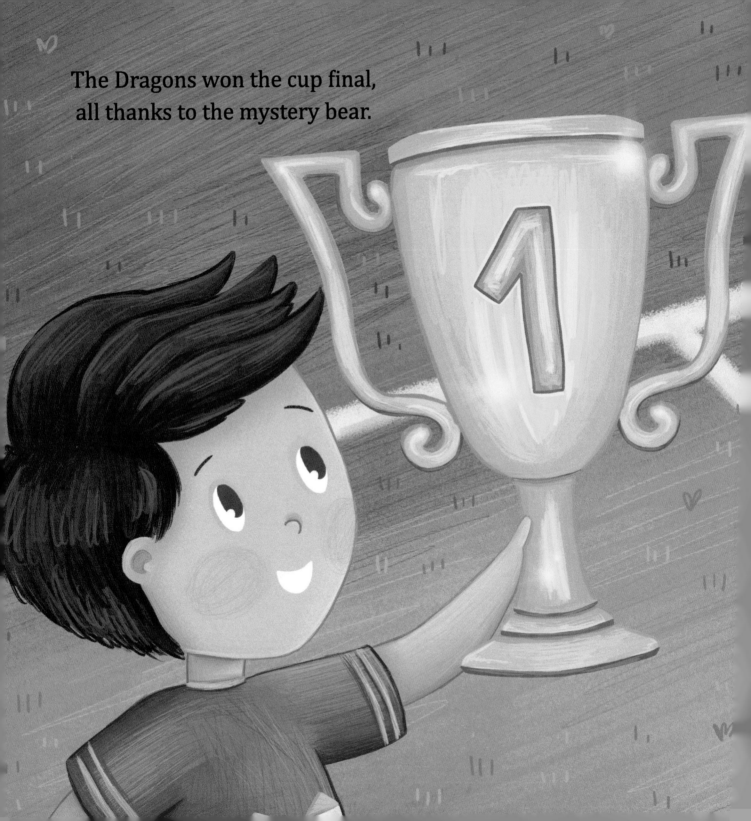

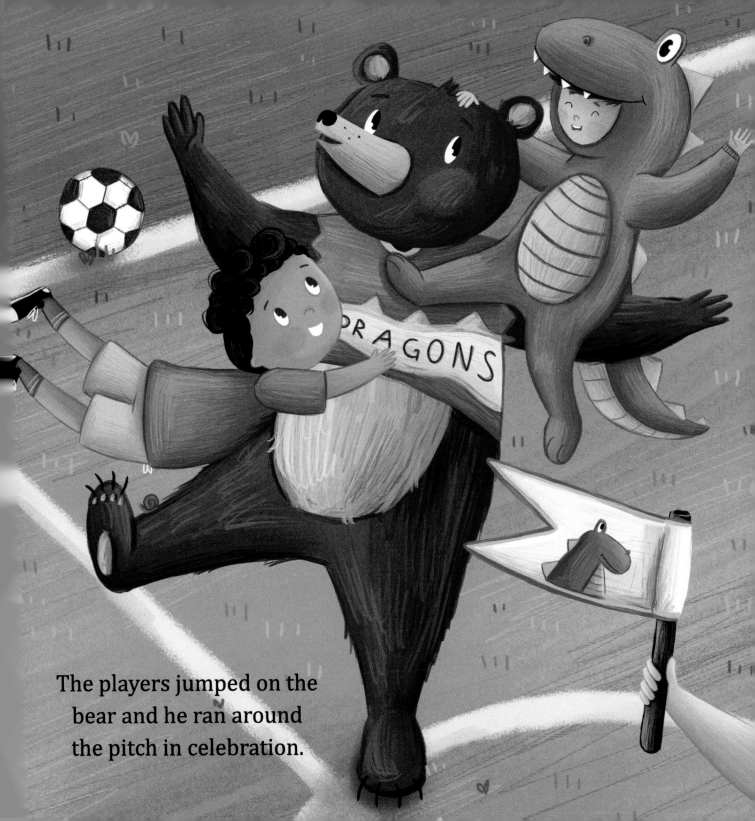

The players jumped on the bear and he ran around the pitch in celebration.

The bear **disappeared** after the match, never to be seen again. In honour of the bear, the Dragons changed their name the following season to...

Made in the USA
Middletown, DE
25 September 2019